THE NIGHT DRAG

DRAGON GIRLS

Rosie the Twilight Dragon

Maddy Mara

DRAGON GIRLS

Rosie the Twilight Dragon

by Maddy Mara

Scholastic Inc.

Copyright © 2022 by Maddy Mara
Illustrations by Barbara Szepesi Szucs, copyright © 2022 by Scholastic Inc.

ISBN 978-1-338-84659-1

10 9 8 7 6 5 4 3 2   22 23 24 25 26

Printed in the U.S.A. 40

First printing 2022

Book design by Stephanie Yang

Rosie rolled out her sleeping bag. The best night of the week had arrived—Friday night was Sleepover Club for Rosie and her best friends, Phoebe and Stella. Rosie woke up every Friday with a quivery feeling bubbling away in her stomach. And the happy bubbles just grew and grew throughout the day. On Sleepover Club nights, anything felt possible.

Today that feeling had been even stronger than usual. Rosie wasn't sure why. She just felt certain that something special was going to happen tonight. It was like the time her friends had thrown a surprise midnight feast for her birthday.

But it wasn't anyone's birthday now. So why was she feeling so excited?

Rosie often found it hard to concentrate at school, but today had been extra hard. She kept thinking about how fun it was going to be tonight. The girls usually baked cookies, and often Rosie would make up a silly bedtime story.

Tonight's sleepover was at Phoebe's house. They stayed at Phoebe's house more often than at Rosie's or Stella's. Phoebe sometimes got homesick, even at friends' houses. So she preferred to be the host. That was fine with Rosie. She loved sleeping at Phoebe's!

Phoebe's family room had a big window with a seat, facing west. The three friends often sat in the window seat, loaded up with bowls of snacks, and watched the sun set. They called it "twilight TV."

Rosie loved watching the sky turn pink, purple, and orange before fading into the rich blues of evening. Her favorite sunsets were when puffy clouds sat low on the horizon. She

often daydreamed about chasing beams of sunlight, or bouncing from cloud to cloud.

"Rosie!" called Phoebe from the family room. "It's almost twilight TV time! Are you coming?"

"Oops, I got distracted!" Rosie called back. "I'll be there in a minute!"

This happened a lot. Rosie would be doing one thing, but then her mind would wander off and she would forget all about what she was supposed to be doing. She hadn't planned to set up her sleeping bag right now. She had been heading to the bathroom to wash her hands!

Rosie glanced outside. There was just the faintest trace of pink in the sky. She jumped up. Twilight was always gone so quickly. She would have to hurry! The bathroom was near Phoebe's bedroom. Rosie liked the bathroom at Phoebe's. It had a soft white mat on the floor and it was filled with plants, including a fern in a macramé pot hanger Phoebe had made herself.

Rosie turned on the taps and picked up the fancy bar of soap resting on the side of the sink. At her house they only had boring, unscented liquid soap. She much preferred the fancy, sweet smelling soap at Phoebe's. It smelled like roses and floated on the water like bubbly clouds.

Rosie looked at the soapy clouds dreamily. Imagine if clouds really did smell like roses! She trailed her finger through the water. And imagine if you could fly around them, like a bird!

As she was daydreaming, Rosie heard a strange sound. It was some sort of song. She had never heard anything so beautiful.

Magic Forest, Magic Forest, come explore...

The voice was very soft and sweet.

"Phoebe? Stella? Is that you?" she called.

No one replied. Maybe it was Phoebe's mom?

But Rosie knew it wasn't her, either. The voice was somehow familiar and completely new at the same time.

Magic Forest, Magic Forest, come explore...

The singing was getting louder. It seemed to be coming from the bubbles in the sink. But that was impossible, right? Rosie looked carefully at the water and noticed something very strange. The pink, foamy soap clouds were getting bigger and puffier.

Then they began to rise up out of the sink!

Rosie glanced around the bathroom. The potted plants were growing bigger, too. Soon they looked more like trees. Rosie's heart began to beat double time. The fizzy feeling in her stomach had been right! Something very special WAS happening.

As the soapy clouds floated into the air, they grew and stretched. The air filled with that delicious rose smell. And even though it was impossible, Rosie was sure she could feel a gentle breeze. She could hear a new line to the song, too.

Magic Forest, Magic Forest, hear my roar!

Rosie did feel like roaring. With excitement! The bathroom was filled with swirling pink clouds. They were so thick that she could not see the bathroom walls. The breeze grew stronger, and the smell of raspberries mixed with the rose scent.

Rosie closed her eyes and stretched out her arms. The breeze wrapped around her, lifting her up into the air and spinning her around. Rosie laughed. It felt a bit like flying! A moment later, the breeze returned her to the ground.

The clouds were still thick, but one thing was very clear. Rosie was no longer in Phoebe's bathroom. But where exactly was she?

2

Gradually, the clouds began to shrink, but the pinkish light was stronger than ever. The scent of fruits and flowers grew more intense, and shapes emerged from the whirling mist.

Rosie glanced around. She was surrounded by trees, their leaves swaying in the breeze. The bathtub had been replaced by a small pond.

When Rosie looked up, the ceiling had disappeared and she found she was gazing instead at the sky. It was painted with the beautiful tones of twilight.

Even the squishy rug that Rosie had been standing on a moment ago felt different. That's because the shaggy white mat had transformed into springy green grass, dotted with little glowing flowers.

Rosie stood in the most amazing forest she had ever seen!

The bathroom wasn't all that had changed. Rosie looked down to see that her legs were covered in shining pink-and-purple scales. Her feet had transformed into powerful-looking claws. Her whole body felt different. Rosie had always been sporty, but right now she felt super strong.

"Whoa!" Rosie gasped. "Something very strange is going on here!"

As she spoke, she got yet another surprise. A burst of glowing purplish light billowed around her face!

"Did I do that?" Rosie wondered aloud.

"Of course you did!" came a little voice from nearby. "And it was a very fine first roar, too, I might add."

Rosie looked around, but no one was there. "Who said that?" she asked.

"I did," said the voice.

This time Rosie spotted a creature hanging upside down from the branch of a tree.

"Ooh, you're so cute! What are you, exactly?" Rosie blurted out.

The animal had the wings of a bat and the face and body of a kitten. "I'm a cat-bat," explained the creature. "My name is GlidyCat. I am SO excited to meet a Night Dragon!"

Rosie felt a surge of excitement. "Night Dragon! What is that?" she asked.

GlidyCat laughed. "YOU are a Night Dragon! Come and look!"

The cat-bat swung off the branch and flittered over to the nearby pond. Rosie followed close behind. Her stomach had never felt so fizzy before. Sure enough, when she looked down into the glassy water, looking back up at her was a magnificent dragon. Pink-and-purple gleaming scales covered her body. On her back sprouted a long, elegant pair of pink-and-purple wings. Beautiful gold swirls spread across her powerful body. She even had a swishy pink-and-purple tail.

Could she really have turned into a DRAGON? There was only one way to know for sure. Rosie opened her mouth, took a deep breath, and roared with all her might. The evening air filled with a purple glow, and the sound echoed through the forest. The trees nearby shook, and the birds twittered in surprise.

Rosie was pretty surprised, too. Surprised, but also proud of herself. She turned to GlidyCat. "What's the difference between a normal dragon and a Night Dragon?" she asked.

"Night Dragons are very special," explained GlidyCat. "They're at their most powerful at night. Plus, they have amazing night vision!"

Rosie thought about this. She did have great eyesight! And it was true that she loved the evening more than any other time of day.

It was almost like GlidyCat could read her mind, because next she said in her silky little voice, "You are the Twilight Dragon. You know all about the dreamy magic of early evening. Plus, you have a very powerful twilight roar. But enough talking! How about you try flying?"

Wow! Rosie hadn't even thought about that! Flying was one of Rosie's favorite daydreams. She couldn't count the number of times she had imagined what it would be like to soar and swoop through the sky. So now, when she gave her wings a flap, it felt completely natural to lift up off the ground. It was like she already knew how to do it!

She grinned. How many times had she gotten in trouble for daydreaming at school? Perhaps it was actually useful after all!

With a couple of strong flaps, Rosie rose

up into the air and began to circle the small clearing. Being in the air felt so freeing! It was wonderful.

GlidyCat flew beside her. "You're a natural!" she purred. "The Tree Queen will be so pleased. You're going to be so helpful on the quest."

Rosie swooped back down to the ground. She had a lot of questions, and she didn't think she could fly and talk at the same time. Not yet, anyway!

"Who is the Tree Queen?" she asked in a rush. "And what quest?"

"The Tree Queen is the ruler of the Magic Forest," GlidyCat explained, grabbing onto a nearby branch with her tail so she was once more hanging upside down.

"Is this amazing place called the Magic Forest?" Rosie asked. The name was so thrilling.

"Yes," GlidyCat purred. "And it's the most wonderful forest! But we must work hard to keep it that way, so the Tree Queen has called you and the other two Night Dragons here to help."

The more GlidyCat said, the more questions Rosie wanted to ask. But GlidyCat let go of the branch and fluttered up into the evening air again.

"Come on, let's get flying. You can ask all your questions when you get to the Tree Queen's glade."

Rosie nodded. "Good idea. It looks like night is going to fall soon. I don't think I'm good enough to fly in the dark yet. I'd probably crash into a tree or something!"

"Nighttime *can't* fall," said GlidyCat, her whiskers twitching. "That's the reason why you are here."

Before Rosie could ask what on earth these mysterious words meant, GlidyCat flew off, out of the clearing.

Rosie flapped her powerful wings, rose up into the air, and followed. Weaving between the trees of the forest at high speed was not easy, but it was fun. Rosie's Night Dragon eyes were perfectly adapted for seeing in the soft evening light.

The only time she had trouble was when a weird bright flare suddenly appeared out of nowhere. Rosie blinked a few times, dazzled. As her eyes adjusted, she saw tiny floating fires. Maybe they were a type of firefly?

Rosie shook her head and kept flying. This was the most exciting thing that had ever happened to her. She was determined not to lose sight of her new little friend GlidyCat.

Finally, they came to another clearing. Here GlidyCat slowed to a stop, and then hovered in midair. Below them glowed a mysterious orb of light. It pulsed with swirling colors.

"What is that?" Rosie whispered in awe.

"That is the force field that protects the Tree Queen's glade," explained GlidyCat. "You must go in there alone. But when you are on your

quest, I will never be far away."

And with that, the little creature disappeared

into the pinky-orange light.

Rosie landed gently on the grass and turned to face the force field. The air shimmered before her. Carefully, she pressed a paw against the glowing screen. It went right through! Rosie could faintly see her paw on the other side. Taking a deep breath and closing her eyes, Rosie walked into the force field. Her scales tingled as she passed through the shining air. It felt like stepping into a magic sunset.

When she opened her eyes, Rosie cried out in delight. She was in the most beautiful glade filled with sweet-smelling flowers and colorful butterflies. Everything glowed gold in the rich twilight. Nearby was a deep pond, its water so clear that Rosie could see jewel-like fish swimming just below the surface.

And there, right in the middle of the glade, grew a magnificent tree. Rosie couldn't stop looking at its branches, laden with rustling leaves and fresh blossoms.

In fact, Rosie was so entranced that it took

her a moment to notice that she wasn't alone.
Two other dragons were in the glade! One
had a crescent moon on her forehead, and
the other had a bright, shining star on hers.
The dragons were also different colors than
Rosie. The moon dragon was the soft, glowing blues and whites of moonlight. The star
dragon was deep purple and gleaming yellow.
Both dragons glimmered in the twilight. They
were looking around in the same amazed way
that Rosie was.

"Hi! Are you Night Dragons?" Rosie called.
"I hope that you guys know what is going on,
because I'm new here."

"Rosie?" the star dragon asked. "It's me, Stella! And this is Phoebe. We just got here as well. Isn't this wild? We're DRAGONS!"

Rosie felt a surge of happiness. There was only one thing better than coming to this magical place and discovering she was a dragon:

discovering that her friends were, too! She rushed over and wrapped a wing over each of them. She figured that was probably how dragons hugged.

"I'm SO happy to see you!" she roared.

"Roaring is fun, isn't it?" Stella laughed.

"It really is," agreed Phoebe. "Almost as good as flying!"

The three friends roared as loudly as they could, until the air was filled with swirling pinks and purples and blues.

Rosie suddenly stopped. "Oops! I just remembered. I was told to come here to meet the Tree Queen. We probably shouldn't be messing around. She might catch us being silly."

Just then, something extraordinary happened. The majestic tree in the center of the glade began to sway back and forth. Its leaves rustled and shook. To Rosie's amazement, the tree began to change. The trunk became a flowing dress, and two of the strong branches transformed into elegant arms.

Moments later, a regal-looking figure appeared before them. Half woman and half tree. Her kind, wise eyes twinkled. "Welcome, Night Dragons," she said in a warm, woody sort of voice. "I am the Tree Queen of the Magic Forest. I am so pleased you are here. And I am delighted to hear that you are so good at roaring. That will be useful on your quest."

Rosie and her friends looked at one another and laughed. The Tree Queen had heard them! She didn't seem upset, though. Rosie felt questions burning inside her. Maybe it wasn't polite to ask questions of a Tree Queen. But Rosie found it impossible to hold them in!

"What IS this quest, exactly?" she asked.

The Tree Queen's face became serious. "You have probably noticed that it is twilight here," she said, her leaves swaying gently.

"Yes! I love this time of day," said Rosie. "It's just always too short."

"Usually it is," agreed the Tree Queen. "But right now, we have the opposite problem. We

are stuck in twilight and cannot move on to night."

"That's weird," said Stella. "Why?"

"It's the work of the Fire Queen and her Fire Sparks," the Tree Queen said.

Rosie shivered. She didn't know who the Fire Queen was, but even her name sounded dangerous. She glanced at her friends. It was clear that they felt the same.

"Who is the Fire Queen?" Phoebe asked nervously.

The Tree Queen looked very serious now. "She is the queen of the hot, dry heat of the day. She hates the cool darkness of the night. But night is important. It's when many plants and creatures of the forest rest and rejuvenate. And it's also when other wonderful creatures are active. Unfortunately, the Fire Queen has become too powerful. She wants to eliminate the night altogether. To do this, she and her helpers, the Fire Sparks, have been destroying the daydreams that filter down from the clouds during the twilight."

This was a lot to take in. But Rosie loved

finding out that daydreams were formed at twilight, her very favorite time of day!

The Tree Queen continued. "Unless the Dream Collectors gather enough daydreams for the following day, the Magic Forest cannot move on to night."

Rosie tried to think about how terrible it would be to have no night. No quiet time to rest for the next day. And worse, no time to dream!

Once again, she found herself brimming with questions. "What are Dream Collectors?" she asked.

"You will find that out very soon, I hope," said the Tree Queen, smiling. "Night Dragons, the first part of your quest is to find the Dream Collectors, and help them."

Rosie and her friends grinned at one another. Rosie couldn't wait to start this adventure, and she knew that Phoebe and Stella felt the same.

"Where do we find them?" asked Phoebe.

"I cannot tell you that, unfortunately," said the Tree Queen. "The Dream Collectors move to wherever the daydreams are falling."

"That's going to make things tricky," said Stella. "I get the feeling the Magic Forest is pretty big."

"It's bigger than you'll ever know," agreed the Tree Queen. "But I can offer you some advice.

Head to where the twilight colors are brightest. And remember to let your own daydreams guide you."

Phoebe and Stella looked puzzled. But Rosie nodded. She loved the idea of being guided by her daydreams!

"Finally, I have something for you," said the Tree Queen.

She began to sway her branches back and forth. Something fell to the ground. Rosie scooped it up. A ball of very fine thread dangled on a delicate silver chain. It was so light and shiny and magical, Rosie wondered if it was made from pure moonlight.

It was beautiful, but Rosie wasn't sure how helpful it would be on a quest.

The Tree Queen seemed to read her mind. "You will find it useful, I promise," she said. "And I know you will do a great job leading this quest, Rosie. Your ability to daydream is exactly what is needed."

Rosie felt like laughing. If there was one thing she was good at, it was daydreaming!

There were about a million other things that Rosie wanted to ask the Tree Queen before they went in search of the Dream Collectors. Like, what should they do if they came across the Fire Queen or her Fire Sparks?

But there was no chance to ask anything more because the queen had turned back into tree form. It was hard to believe this tree, with its silvery leaves and strong trunk, had looked like a person just moments ago.

Rosie took the silver chain and draped it around her neck like a necklace. She turned to her friends. "Looks like we're on our own!" she said. "Are you Dragon Girls ready?"

Stella nodded. "I am SO ready," she said.

"We've totally got this," agreed Phoebe. She was the shyer, more nervous one of the group, but even she was bursting to go on an adventure!

Together, the three friends stepped back through the protective force field. Outside the glade, the sky was just as pink and orange as it had been before. It was as if the forest was holding its breath, waiting for a night that might never arrive.

"Right. Let's fly!" said Rosie, flapping her wings and rising into the air.

Stella and Phoebe joined her. They weren't as good as Rosie at flying yet. They kept bumping into each other and laughing. But to Rosie, flying felt like something she was born to do.

"The Tree Queen said we should head to where the twilight colors are brightest," remembered Phoebe. "Where is that?"

"Let's go up above the trees so we can see more," Rosie suggested. She led the way up through the treetops. It was the highest she'd ever flown! Down below, the Magic Forest stretched away in all directions. The setting sun glowed on the horizon, lighting up the trees in twilight tones. The leaves shone like they were made from liquid gold.

"That's where we need to go," she said, pointing a wing toward the bright horizon.

As she spoke, a thread from the silver ball Rosie wore began to uncoil. It stretched out toward the colorful spot where Rosie had pointed.

She laughed in surprise. "The magic thread agrees!" she said.

Rosie had daydreamed many times about flying with her friends. She had pictured them all swooping and doing tumble turns together. But she had never really thought it would happen.

"I feel like I should pinch myself," she called to Phoebe and Stella. "But now that I have these big claws, I guess that's probably not a great idea!"

"True!" Stella laughed. "But hey, how about we try holding paws and flying?"

The friends linked paws and flew together. It was tricky to fly this way, but it was fun. It was so fun that Rosie almost forgot that they were on a quest. Then she felt the ball of thread tugging down on the chain around her neck.

Rosie looked. Down below, a patch of forest glowed more intensely pink and orange than anywhere else. Rosie knew that this was where they should go.

"Get ready for landing," she called to the others.

"I hope I do better than my first time," called Stella. "I ended upside down in a bush!"

"Remember to put your talons forward and your wings back," Rosie advised as the air whooshed past. She aimed for a small clearing in the trees. Her heart pounded with excitement.

What were Dream Collectors, exactly? Rosie

imagined huge beasts, with arms that scraped the sky with their massive claws. She just hoped they were *friendly* huge beasts!

Gracefully, Rosie landed on the soft grass. Phoebe skidded to a stop beside her.

"Watch out!" yelled Stella as she bounced clumsily along the ground. She tumbled a couple of times and then finally came to a stop just before a bush. "I didn't land in a tree this time!" She grinned, getting up and looking at the others. "That's a definite improvement."

Suddenly, a chorus of small but firm voices rang through the air. "Stand by! Incoming daydream!"

The surrounding trees began to shake and

shiver. What was happening? Then Rosie spotted little creatures with long tails and fluffy orange tufts on the tips of their ears, scurrying up and down the trunks of the trees. That's what was making them shake! Her friends had spotted the animals, too.

"Are they squirrels?" wondered Phoebe.

"Their tails are too long," Stella said.

"We're Dream Collectors," squeaked one of them as it ran by with its nose pointed to the sky. "And we're really busy right now. A new batch of daydreams has just dropped."

Rosie looked up. At first she couldn't see anything. But as she studied the sky, she could just make out what appeared to be bubbles.

They were all different shapes and sizes, and they were drifting down toward them.

The Dream Collectors scurried back and forth, moving into position.

"Get ready to catch!" they called to one another.

"Don't let them touch the ground or they will burst!"

"Let's hope that the Fire Sparks don't get them this time!"

The Fire Sparks? Rosie shivered. The Tree Queen had said the Fire Sparks worked with the Fire Queen. Were they here?

The bubbles were almost at ground level now. Some of the Dream Collectors ran back up the trees, reaching out their little paws in readiness. As a bubble drifted close to Rosie, she could see small scenes inside them. One showed a field of flowers, laden with pollen. Another showed a huge pile of fresh carrots.

"They're different creatures' daydreams," said a familiar voice. "Daydreams for bees, daydreams for rabbits. And many others."

Rosie turned and saw GlidyCat by her side. "After the Dream Collectors have caught them, they scamper around, hiding the bubbles around the forest. When creatures find them, the bubbles shatter and release the daydream."

"They're beautiful!" Rosie sighed.

She reached out to catch one, but before the bubble touched her outstretched paw, a loud, angry buzzing filled the air.

From beyond the trees, Rosie saw fiercely burning lights. There were just a few at first, but then more and more appeared. They swirled in a mass, crackling like electricity. The lights surged through the trees and into the clearing. They buzzed and jumped around like embers blown by the wind. Fire Sparks! They were so hot and bright that Rosie had to turn away. Besides, just looking at them made her feel oddly cranky.

When she glanced back, she saw something terrible. One of the sparks landed on a daydream bubble. The bubble glowed red hot for a moment, then exploded.

"Oh no!" cried one of the Dream Collectors. "It's happening again! The sparks are destroying the daydreams. If we don't have enough of them in place for tomorrow, night will not fall."

Rosie looked at her friends. No words were needed. They all knew what they had to do.

Together, the Night Dragons rose into the air. There was no way they were going to let the Fire Sparks destroy the forest's daydreams!

Rosie, Phoebe, and Stella flew into the mass of swirling sparks. The glowing points stung as they touched Rosie's scales, but she barely noticed. How dare the Fire Sparks destroy these precious daydreams!

She zoomed among the glowing lights,

swishing at them with her tail. The sparks scattered, but then they returned and popped the bubbles, one after another.

Rosie felt her frustration building. How could they stop these Fire Sparks? They were making her so mad!

"They want to make you angry. Try roaring instead," purred GlidyCat in Rosie's ear.

Rosie thought of the Tree Queen's comment that their roars would be helpful. Yes! Roaring was exactly what she needed to do. She took a big breath and roared out her frustration with all her might.

The air shimmered with a purple-blue mist. It smelled like all the wonderful purple things that Rosie loved. Plums, lavender, passion fruit, and, of course, dragon fruit.

"That's working, Rosie!" called Stella from the other side of the clearing. "Look!"

All the nearby sparks had been extinguished by Rosie's roar. But it wasn't long before more sparks appeared and began attacking the bubbles once again.

"Let's roar together," suggested Phoebe.

Rosie nodded, and on the count of three, the friends roared so loudly that the leaves of the surrounding trees shook! A powerful mist swirled through the clearing, so thick that Rosie couldn't see through it.

When the air settled, Rosie looked around.

The Fire Sparks were gone! Her angry feelings had vanished, too. And down on the forest floor, the Dream Collectors were hurrying to gather the remaining bubbles before they touched the ground.

Rosie flew lower, landing carefully between the bubbles. Her friends landed beside her. This time Stella barely skidded at all.

GlidyCat came to rest on Rosie's shoulder.

"We did it!" cried Stella. "We got rid of the Fire Sparks. So now night can fall, right?"

"Wrong!" squeaked one of the Dream Collectors. It scurried over to Rosie with a daydream bubble balanced on the tip of its monkey-like tail. "Look!"

Rosie peered into the bubble. Instead of a beautiful daydream, she saw gray clouds and drizzle. Rosie was pretty sure no one ever day-dreamed about dull drizzling days.

"What's happened?" she asked.

"Daydreams are very delicate," explained the Dream Collector. "If they get blown around or shaken too much, they become muddled and sad."

"Oh no!" Phoebe groaned. "So we didn't save them?"

Another little Dream Collector bounded over. "They can be fixed," it said. "They will just need to be returned to the daydream maker for repairs."

"What kind of creature is a daydream maker?" asked Phoebe curiously.

The Dream Collectors laughed.

"It's not a creature at all," explained one.

"It's a place where daydreams are made. It's up on the first layer of clouds, known as the Hope Clouds," said another Dream Collector.

Stella pulled a face at Rosie, who knew exactly what she was thinking. A daydream maker up in the clouds sounded even more impossible than one in the forest! But everything in the Magic Forest seemed surprising and wonderful.

"Well, at least we have wings," said Stella.

"We can fly up there with the daydreams that need fixing."

"Dragons can't fly that high," said one of the Dream Collectors. "The air is too thin for you. But cloud folk have no trouble."

"So how do we get up there?" asked Rosie.

"You must ride a sunset ray," said the Dream Collector. "And the good news is the ray station is not far from here."

"But the bad news for us is that the ray stationmaster is very grumpy," continued another Dream Collector, wringing its little paws together. "He doesn't let just anyone catch a sunset ray."

Rosie decided not to worry about this. Besides, another problem had just occurred to her. How were they going to carry the daydream bubbles? They were so precious! And the Night Dragons didn't have a bag. There was no way they could fly carrying all those bubbles.

As she was thinking, Rosie felt the silver thread on the chain twitch. It had begun to wiggle back and forth, like a worm trying to escape. An idea struck her.

Quickly, she unlooped the chain from around her neck. Using her sharp dragon teeth, she nipped off long sections of the fine thread. It seemed to be endlessly long.

"What are you doing?" asked Stella.

"Let's make a net out of this thread," Rosie said. "Maybe it could be like those macramé hangers you make for plants, Phoebe? Then we'll scoop up all the daydreams and carry them that way."

Phoebe grinned. "Great idea," she said.

Rosie, Stella, and Phoebe set to work, weaving a huge net. Rosie was worried it would take a long time to make, but Phoebe took the lead on the project, teaching the others. Even better, the thread seemed to learn what they were doing and soon started weaving itself into perfect knots.

In next to no time, the Night Dragons had

created the perfect net. It was light but very strong.

"It looks great!" said the Dream Collectors, clapping their little paws together delightedly. "We'll help you gather them up." They scampered around, collecting the bubbles. They were experts at transporting them, balancing several on their tails at one time.

Rosie didn't dare carry more than one bubble. They were so fragile that she worried her sharp claws would pop them.

Finally, every last bubble was carefully loaded into the net. Rosie, Phoebe, and Stella gently gathered up the ends and brought them together at the top.

Rosie secured the net, leaving three lengths of thread dangling. She still had plenty of thread around her neck, even though the bundle was huge!

"It looks kind of heavy," said Phoebe.

Rosie took the three threads and handed one

to each of her friends, wrapping the third one around her paw.

"Let's test it and see," she said.

The Night Dragons rose into the air. The bundle rose, too. And then it kept rising. The bubble-filled net was soon hovering above the Dragon Girls like a hot-air balloon.

"I guess daydreams are light!" Rosie grinned. "Even the ones that are a bit sad and muddled."

"They are light at the moment," agreed one of the Dream Collectors. "But they will get heavier over time. Don't take too long getting there!"

"Also, they might explode," added another Dream Collector. "So be careful!"

"Goodbye, Dream Collectors!" Rosie called. "We'll get these daydreams fixed, don't worry."

The little creatures scampered up the surrounding trees and waved their paws. "Good luck, Night Dragons," they called. "Hopefully the ray stationmaster is in a good mood today."

The Dragon Girls flew above the treetops.

The twilight was as bright as ever. GlidyCat fluttered by Rosie's side.

"Which way should we go?" Phoebe asked.

"If we're riding a sunset ray," Stella said, "I guess we head for the sunset?"

Rosie looked around. It was simple in theory, but the entire sky was filled with sunset rays at the moment.

"Let the daydreams guide you there," said GlidyCat. "They know the way."

GlidyCat was right! Rosie could feel the daydreams gently tugging in their net.

The group flew in silence for a while. Rosie's mind was filled with questions. Would they recognize the ray station when they saw it? And what would they do if the stationmaster didn't want to let them ride a ray up to the daydream maker?

But Rosie shook away the worries. *We'll find a way*, she told herself firmly. She knew that she and her friends could do just about anything together.

"Am I imagining it, or is the sky getting brighter?" Stella asked suddenly.

"I was just wondering the same thing," said Phoebe.

Rosie looked around. The sky did seem brighter! It was almost like the sun was rising.

But that was impossible! It was evening, and night hadn't even fallen yet. Also, there was something odd about the glow.

Rosie looked down. The strange light moved across the trees below her, like tiny flames. As she watched, the light began to spread. It came toward Rosie and her friends.

"Fire Sparks!" yelled Rosie. "And they're heading this way!"

But it was too late. In a flash, they were surrounded by a twisting mass of sharp little flares. Rosie lashed at them with her tail and swiped them away with her claws. It was like being swarmed by evil fairy lights! Her frustration returned, even stronger than before.

"Don't forget your roar, Rosie," urged GlidyCat.

But roaring while flying and carrying a huge bundle of daydreams was very difficult! The Night Dragons did their best, but they just couldn't seem to roar strongly enough to put out the Fire Sparks.

"Watch out," called Phoebe. "There's a rain cloud up there! Should we go above or below it?"

A gray cloud loomed ahead. It wasn't very big, but it looked dark and heavy with rain. Rosie was about to swoop below it when she had an idea.

"Let's fly through it!" Rosie called to her friends, swishing away a cluster of Fire Sparks with her tail.

Phoebe and Stella looked surprised but nodded. Although the Fire Sparks were making Rosie feel all grouchy and itchy, she managed to smile. It was so good to know that her friends trusted her! As they approached the rain cloud,

Rosie held on tightly to the silvery cord of the net. It would be terrible if she accidentally let go and the daydreams blew away.

The sparks swarmed around them as they flew into the cloud. The light grew dim, and Rosie felt like she was wrapped in a big, wet towel.

She heard a strange, angry hissing sound. Uh-oh, was that the daydreams? Was the rain cloud damaging them?

Then Rosie sighed with relief. It wasn't the daydreams fizzing out. It was the sound of the sparks going out! Her plan had worked! By the time the Night Dragons flew out the other side of the cloud, all the stinging little fires were gone.

Even better, the net was still intact. They had not lost a single daydream bubble.

"We did it!" roared Rosie triumphantly. "High five? Er, maybe a low tail?"

Laughing, Rosie, Phoebe, and Stella swung their tails around and tried to smack them together. They missed the first two tries, but finally managed it!

GlidyCat nuzzled Rosie's cheek. "Well done," she purred. "You dealt with those sparks perfectly. The ray station is just down there, so I will leave you for now. But I'll be back if you need me."

And with that, the little cat-bat fluttered off into the glowing forest below.

Rosie felt the magic of the net tugging gently. The daydreams were sinking lower!

Looking down, Rosie saw a very strange thing. Reaching up from between the trees were three polished metal archways, shining like burnished gold. They stretched high into the sky, disappearing into the clouds up above. Sunset rays!

A comforting heat radiated from the rays, like concrete after a sunny day.

"This must be the ray station," Rosie called to her friends. "Let's go find the stationmaster."

With the net of daydreams leading the way, the Night Dragons drifted slowly down. As they landed on the floor of the forest, something fluttered up to Rosie. Had GlidyCat returned?

Sadly, no. Before her was a large pink-and-brown moth with a soft, fuzzy body. It had impressively long and curly antennae and an extremely grumpy expression.

"Hello! Are you the ray stationmaster, by any chance?" Rosie asked politely.

"Yes, I am," replied the moth. "What are you doing here? I have just polished up the rays with my wings, and now you three come along, dropping dragon dust all over them."

"We didn't drop anything on them!" said Stella hotly.

Rosie shot her friend a warning look. She knew how much Stella hated it when people were mean, but they had to be as nice as possible to this moth.

"Sorry about that! We'd like to ride a ray up to the daydream maker," explained Rosie.

"I only let those with very good reasons travel on the rays," said the moth sniffily.

"We HAVE a very good reason," said Rosie. "See all these daydream bubbles? They are damaged and need to be repaired. Until they are fixed, evening cannot fall in the Magic Forest."

The moth conductor curled and uncurled his antennae thoughtfully. "Hmm. That is a good reason," the moth agreed. "Okay, you may ride a ray."

Rosie beamed at her friends. She had thought that this was going to be much harder!

But the moth raised one of his six legs into the air. "However! Only ONE of you may travel. And then there is the question of payment."

"Question of payment?" Phoebe repeated, looking worried.

"You can't charge us!" Stella spluttered. "We don't have any money. And anyway, we're trying to help the forest!"

"Nonetheless, payment is required," the stationmaster said flatly. "Isn't that right, conductor?"

There was a fluttering of wings, and another moth slid down one of the rays, jumping off onto a nearby branch at the last moment.

The second moth looked just like a smaller version of the stationmaster, except for one important thing. He was smiling.

"Hi!" he said cheerily. "Do you want to use the ray?"

"Yes, please," said Rosie. "We really need to. But the stationmaster has said that we need to pay?"

The little moth waved his antennae around. "Don't mind Dad," he whispered. "He looks grumpy, but he's actually a total softy."

Rosie wasn't quite sure she believed this. "How much does it cost to ride a ray?" she asked.

The little moth coughed and then spoke in an official-sounding voice. "The cost of riding is one bedtime story."

The Night Dragons looked at one another

in delight. This was the kind of payment they could definitely afford!

"It has to be an excellent story, though," warned the little moth. "Which one of you is going to tell it?"

"That's easy," said Stella. "It HAS to be you, Rosie."

Phoebe nodded. "You're the best storyteller," she said to Rosie. "And you love doing it, right?"

Rosie smiled, but she felt a bit nervous. It was true that she loved making up stories. But usually she did it just for fun. She'd never had to invent one that mattered so much!

The bigger moth fluttered over and came to rest in front of her. He crossed two legs impatiently. "Well?" he said. "We can't wait all day, you know."

"It's not like nighttime is about to fall anytime soon," muttered Stella.

Rosie thought fast. She often put her friends into the stories she told at their sleepovers. They always seemed to enjoy that. Maybe the moths would like it, too?

It was worth a try.

"Once upon a time, there were two moths," she began. "They were beautiful brown-and-pink moths, and they lived together in the special place where the rays of sunset lifted up to the sky."

The little moth fluttered his wings excitedly. "Just like us, Dad!"

The younger moth leaned forward, listening intently. Even the grumpy dad moth seemed interested.

Rosie closed her eyes and let the story flow out of her. Often when Rosie was telling a story, it didn't really feel like she was making it up at all. It was more like she was unfurling the story that was rolled up inside her.

This story was like that. It was about a brave

little moth and his dad, who were going to a midnight ball on the moon. Their wings were specially painted with stardust so they would shine brightly in the pale light. Some friendly Night Dragons gave the moths a lift up to the moon. Then the moths danced so beautifully, they were made the king and prince of the Midnight Moon Ball.

While she was talking, Rosie almost forgot where she was. This happened when she was telling a story. She got so lost in it that she didn't think about anything else but the tale itself.

When she finished, she slowly opened one

eye and then the other. It all came flooding
back. She was a Night Dragon in the Magic
Forest. And she was telling a grumpy moth
and his son a story in exchange for a trip to
the daydream maker.

"That was great!" said the little moth, fluttering happily. "Don't you think, Dad?"

The bigger moth sat very still, his six legs all clasped together before him.

"It...was...beautiful." He sighed. His voice sounded quite different. Instead of grouchy, the moth now sounded peaceful and relaxed. "I haven't heard a story like that since I was a caterpillar." He gave a huge yawn and stretched two of his legs. "It has made me very sleepy. I'm going to have a little nap now."

"So, can I catch one of the rays?" Rosie asked.

"You sure can! Hop on," said the little moth cheerfully. "I'll take you up right away."

"You're going to leave?" said the dad moth,

yawning. "Wouldn't you like to stay and tell more stories?"

"Sorry, but we need to get these daydreams repaired," said Rosie firmly. "Daydreaming is where stories come from, after all. If we run out of daydreams, there won't be any more stories."

That woke the moth up. He sprang to his feet—all six of them.

"Quickly then, Mothew!" he said, calling to the smaller moth. "Take this Night Dragon up to the daydream maker. You know the way, don't you?"

"Absolutely!" said Mothew proudly.

He flew over to where the gleaming rays

rose from the treetops. The Night Dragons followed behind.

Rosie gasped. From a distance, the rays looked very steady and still. But now that she was up close, Rosie saw that was not the case. The rays were in motion, like a sort of magical escalator. Only they were MUCH faster than any escalator Rosie had ever been on!

"I'm a little nervous," Rosie admitted to Mothew, looking up at the fast-moving rays.

"Don't be," said the little moth. "Just hold on to the sides, and don't let go. We will be traveling very fast and very high."

Rosie gulped. This was not very reassuring!

Stella and Phoebe handed her the other strings holding the net of daydreams together.

"Don't let go of this, either," said Stella. "It would be terrible if the daydreams escaped while you were on your way up."

"And hopefully you can find where to get them fixed as soon as possible. They're looking even murkier now," added Phoebe.

Phoebe was right. The images inside the bubbles were no longer visible at all. They were completely covered by a thick, murky mist.

Rosie started to feel really worried. If only her friends were coming with her! But there was no time to think about that right now. She had to focus on catching this ray. It sped by at top speed. Rosie had a bad feeling that she might slip off when she tried to climb on board.

The net of daydreams pulled gently as she moved toward the ray. They were definitely getting heavier and sadder.

Rosie took a deep breath. She was going to do this, no matter what.

With a beat of her wings, Rosie leapt up and landed on the closest ray. Instantly, she began to whoosh up into the sky. It was kind of like surfing, but in the air.

Mothew jumped on behind her. "Off we go!" he called. "I'll take you to the head cloud. Someone there will be able to help you, I'm sure."

The ray of light was warm and smooth

beneath Rosie's claws, like a slide on a hot day. The strangest thing was that she felt like she was sticking to it, almost like a magnet. It was odd, but at least it didn't feel like she was going to fall off.

Rosie felt a flash of excitement as she zoomed up. She was heading to the clouds! She had often imagined creatures living up there. In fact, Rosie had created whole cloud cities in her mind during boring classes at school. But she never really, truly thought it was possible.

"We're halfway there!" announced Mothew. "Watch out, we start going *really* fast now."

Rosie was about to ask if it was possible to

go faster than they already were. But before she could speak, the ray leapt forward. It was like it had moved into a new gear! They were now traveling more swiftly than ever.

Faster and faster they went, speeding toward the puffy clouds above. The higher they traveled, the harder it was to breathe deeply.

Rosie started to feel a little dizzy. Bright lights swam before her eyes. Was that because of the thin air?

"Fire Sparks!" shouted Mothew.

With a shiver, Rosie saw that Mothew was right. The lights were Fire Sparks. And looking down, Rosie saw that hundreds more were swarming up the sunset ray toward her!

GlidyCat whooshed into view. The little cat-bat always turned up when Rosie was in trouble!

She heard GlidyCat's voice in her ear. "Rosie, focus! Try not to lose your temper. And whatever you do, don't let go of the ray!"

Again, Rosie wished her friends were here. How was she going to fight these sparks on her own?

Rosie held on tight as the gleaming sparks chased her on the ray, crackling loudly and burning so brightly that it was hard to see. She swished at the sparks with her tail, trying to get them out of her way. But it was no good. There were just too many Fire Sparks swarming around the net of daydream bubbles.

Rosie felt hot and annoyed. The Fire Sparks always made her feel like that. But honestly, it would be terrible to get this far only to have the bubbles destroyed before she could get them to the daydream maker!

She tried to roar, but the air was so thin that her roar came out pale and weak. It only put out a handful of the sparks.

"I'll help!" GlidyCat called, and she zoomed around, beating at the sparks with her wings.

"Me too!" Mothew shouted, trying to do the same with his tiny moth wings.

It was kind and brave of them both, but they were very small creatures, and there were a lot of sparks.

"I *wish* Phoebe and Stella were here," Rosie groaned. She just knew that together they'd be able to figure out what to do.

"Coming right up!" called a cheery voice.

It sounded like Stella, but that wasn't possible, was it? They were still down below! Gripping on to the sunset ray as tightly as she could, Rosie looked down.

There, in the distance, were Stella and Phoebe! They were zooming up the other two rays toward her!

The Fire Sparks buzzed angrily. They clearly weren't happy to see the other Night Dragons. In fact, they were so loud that when Phoebe shouted something, Rosie couldn't make out

the words properly. It sounded like Phoebe had said, "Daydream your way through."

Phoebe and Stella were traveling fast, but they were still a long way down.

Just then, Rosie heard another noise. It was one of the daydream bubbles popping. Oh no! She watched in horror as its silvery dust floated away on the wind.

Moments later, another popped.

And another.

Rosie had to do something, and she had to do it now! She thought about what Phoebe had said. Or what she *thought* Phoebe had said. *Daydream your way through?*

Maybe if she imagined herself getting through the swarm of Fire Sparks, she actually *would* get through.

Rosie wasn't at all sure this would work. *But I am in the Magic Forest*, Rosie reminded herself. *Just about anything is possible here!*

Swishing her tail one more time at the mass of crackling Fire Sparks, Rosie closed her eyes.

She pictured herself putting her head down and pushing through the sparks at top speed. She imagined GlidyCat and Mothew with her, as well as her besties. They were all zooming up the sunset rays, side by side, until they arrived safely at the daydream maker.

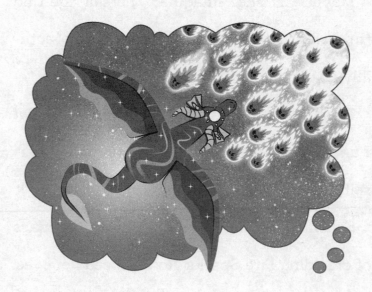

It was a great daydream and it felt weirdly real. Rosie opened her eyes. Somehow, she knew what to do.

I am the Twilight Dragon, she reminded herself. *And I'm on a sunset ray, which is most powerful and magical at twilight.*

She took a deep breath and roared as loudly as she could. This was *her* roar, brimming with twilight power. It swirled and twirled in the most beautiful pinks and purples and a hint of yellow. The roar hit the bright, shining gold of the sunset ray and bounced off it again, like a ball of pure Night Dragon energy. The sunset ray had made Rosie's roar even stronger!

The roar surrounded the angry Fire Sparks so that Rosie could no longer see them. She heard fizzing sounds, like a candle being snuffed out. As the mist cleared, Rosie looked around. She couldn't see a single Fire Spark! She'd destroyed them!

Up ahead floated a huge, puffy white cloud. The cloud's edges were tinged with gold from the sun. Rosie somehow knew it was the cloud she was looking for. She raced along the ray, GlidyCat and Mothew by her side.

"You did it!" cried a voice.

"We knew you would!" added another one.

Rosie knew those voices. Looking back, she saw Phoebe and Stella right behind her!

"Thanks for the daydreaming tip!" she called as they all whooshed along together. "How did you know?"

"Mothew's dad told us," Stella said.

"He's our new best friend," Phoebe explained when Rosie looked confused.

It was only then that Rosie spotted the brown-and-pink moth perched on Phoebe's shoulder. He didn't look grumpy anymore. In fact, he was smiling just like his son!

Rosie had so many questions, she didn't know where to start. But it's very hard to think straight when you're whooshing along a sunset ray at top speed, high in the air.

"It felt wrong watching you head off on your

own," explained Stella. "So we made a deal with Mothew's dad. We told him another story, and he let us catch a ray!"

Rosie tried not to burst out laughing. Stella was brilliant at convincing people to do things. It was kind of her superpower!

"I've never had such an adventure before," said the dad moth excitedly. "And look, Son! We're almost at the daydream maker now."

"We sure are, Dad. Get ready to disembark, Night Dragons," said Mothew in his official voice.

The puffy white-and-gold cloud loomed up ahead, and the ray looked like it went straight through the middle of it.

GlidyCat purred in Rosie's ear. "You're going to be fine now. I'll see you again soon!"

"You're not coming?" cried Rosie. She somehow felt better with GlidyCat by her side.

"You will be fine. You have your friends here." Waving a wing in goodbye, GlidyCat flew off back toward the forest.

"Hold on!" warned Mothew. "This part can be bumpy."

As they entered the cloud, Rosie gripped the ray even more tightly. A cold wind whipped around her, pushing her from side to side. She could hear the daydream bubbles rattling together in their net.

"It sure is bumpy!" yelled Stella from her ray.

She sounded like she was enjoying it, which made Rosie grin. Stella always wanted to go on the scariest rides at any amusement park. Flying through a windy cloud would be nothing to her!

Rosie wasn't quite as enthusiastic about scary rides, and she was glad when they popped out the other side.

"Wow!" Phoebe gasped as the Dragon Girls climbed off their sunset rays and stepped onto the thick layer of cloud. "This place is amazing!"

The cloud stretched as far as Rosie could see. She had flown above the clouds in a plane before, but this was very different. It felt like visiting a new land—where everything was made of clouds! Nearby grew a puffy tree, and off in the distance loomed a big puffy mountain. Rosie took a cautious step forward.

She knew that clouds in the normal world were made of water droplets. There was no way you could walk on that! But the clouds here seemed to be made of something more like snow, although it wasn't cold. Even better, it was also slightly springy! But just *how* springy was it?

There was only one way to find out. Rosie tried jumping on the clouds. It was like bouncing on the best trampoline ever! The moment they saw her do this, Stella and Phoebe just *had* to join in, too, and soon all three Night Dragons were leaping around on the cloud.

"Great jumping, Night Dragons," said the dad moth. "But don't you have a job to do?"

Rosie stopped jumping right away. "Oops, you're right," she said.

"Have you noticed that the clouds keep changing shape?" asked Phoebe.

"Yes!" said Rosie, gazing about in wonder. "That cloud over there was shaped like a strawberry bush doing yoga. Now it looks like a turtle driving a car."

"That's right," said Mothew, fluttering up above the group. "Everything changes here all the time. The only thing that doesn't change its shape is the head cloud."

"That's where we're going?" Rosie asked.

"We sure are," said Mothew. "That's where the Sky Skimmers make the daydream bubbles."

Rosie and her friends beamed at one another. This was great news!

"Mothew, what does the head cloud look like?" Rosie asked, eager to get going.

In this place, anything could be shaped like anything. Even the all-important head cloud.

"I just told you!" Mothew grinned, sounding surprised. "It's shaped like a head."

Rosie burst out laughing. "Oh! I thought you meant it was the main cloud," she said.

"It IS the main cloud," said Mothew, looking more puzzled than ever. "And it's shaped like a head. Look, it's over there."

Rosie looked where Mothew's antennae were pointing. Sure enough, there was a huge cloud that looked a lot like a head.

"I can see things moving," said Phoebe. "They're soft and white and floaty."

"Sky Skimmers," Mothew explained. "Come on, everyone."

Like the Night Dragons, the moths couldn't fly in the thin air, but Mothew was an expert at hopping over the bouncy cloud surface.

Although the Dragon Girls were much bigger, it was hard for Rosie, Phoebe, and Stella to keep up. It was fun but not easy!

The dad moth decided to catch a ride on Rosie's back. It only took a few big leaps for the group to arrive at the head cloud, and as they approached, the mouth opened and something fluffy and white floated out.

"Look at that little cloud!" Stella exclaimed. "It's got eyes!"

The cloudlike thing seemed hurt. "I am not a little cloud," it said. "I am a fully grown Sky Skimmer."

"Sorry," said Stella, trying not to laugh.

The Sky Skimmer had an unexpectedly deep voice!

Rosie leaned her head down toward the Sky Skimmer. "We need your help," she explained. "As you probably know, the Magic Forest is stuck in a never-ending twilight. The daydream bubbles you're sending down keep getting damaged by the Fire Sparks."

"I know. And it's a real problem because we cannot make any new daydreams." The Sky Skimmer sighed. "The material we make daydreams from grows overnight. We need night to fall so we can grow more."

This was bad news! Without the daydreams

being scattered by the Dream Collectors, night would never fall!

Rosie showed the Sky Skimmer the net of daydreams. "These are the only ones left," she said. "They've been damaged by the Fire Sparks. Do you think you can fix them?"

The Sky Skimmer floated around the daydream bubbles, inspecting them closely. The group waited anxiously.

"Yes, we can fix these," it finally announced. "But we must act fast. Follow me!" With that, the Sky Skimmer disappeared into the head cloud.

Quickly, the Dragon Girls leapt into the mouth of the head cloud and followed the little cloudy creature as best they could.

The head cloud seemed much bigger on the inside than it looked on the outside, and the girls had to hurry to keep up with the Sky Skimmer.

The Night Dragons bounced through one fluffy white passageway after another, their paws sinking into the soft clouds with every step.

"I feel like I'm running a race, but with pillows for shoes," commented Stella.

Eventually, the Sky Skimmer stopped in a large, airy space. Before them was the strangest-looking cloud Rosie had ever seen. It looked like a machine. Long white pipe shapes twisted and wiggled around one another like the most complicated knot in the world.

"Bring one of the daydreams over," called the Sky Skimmer, landing like a feather near one of the pipes.

Rosie bounced over with one of the daydream bubbles from the net.

The skimmer looked stormy and gray suddenly. "It's even cloudier than before," it said. "The machine might not be able to repair it."

Rosie jutted out her chin. "We're so close now, it *has* to work!" she said. "Let's at least try."

"Yes, we can try!" agreed the Sky Skimmer. It pursed its lips and began to blow. The bubble rose up, and then, with a whoosh, it disappeared into the pipe!

Rosie shut her eyes. She had no idea how the

cloud machine worked, but she could imagine it. She pictured the daydream rushing through the twisting pipes, being polished up by the soft cloudy lining. She imagined it stopping for a moment and maybe a small bird inside the machine pecking at the surface to make a tiny hole.

In her mind, Rosie saw the damaged dream dripping out. Then she conjured up another bird, bending over the bubble and singing a new daydream into it. Finally, she imagined an extra-fluffy cloud polishing the bubble's surface and sealing up the little hole.

It was only her imagination, of course, but it felt real. Rosie was sure that the cloud machine had done its job!

The cloud pipes began to shiver and shake.

"It's almost finished!" cheeped the Sky Skimmer. "Come around this side!"

The group hurried over to the cloud pipe at the back of the machine, where the Sky Skimmer now floated.

"Hold out your paws!" instructed the Sky Skimmer.

Rosie did as she was told, and just in time! A second later, the bubble dropped into her waiting paws. It felt warm, like bread fresh from the oven. Its surface shone like a Christmas ornament.

"Did it work? Is the daydream fixed?" asked Phoebe nervously.

Rosie held it up for everyone to see. The murkiness had vanished. Now the bubble contained a tiny scene of the Magic Forest, bathed in moonlight. The sky in the bubble blazed with stars.

Mothew did three excited loops in the air. "It worked!" he yelled in his fuzzy moth voice.

Rosie wanted to do some excited loops, too. But loops would have to wait. There was more work to do.

She held up the remaining bundle of damaged bubbles. "All right! Let's get the rest of these daydreams fixed!"

Phoebe and Stella began feeding the bubbles into the cloud machine while Rosie caught the cleaned ones at the other end and carefully returned them to the net.

Mothew flew back and forth excitedly, shouting encouraging words. "You're nearly done, Dragon Girls! The daydreams look better than ever."

It was true. Every daydream bubble shone brightly, with a happy scene moving inside it. They released a warm, sweet smell, like a baking cake. Rosie knew that the creatures of the Magic Forest were going to enjoy bumping into them.

As the net filled with the cleaned daydreams, it slowly began to rise. It was like the net was filled with puffy hope.

Finally, the machine let out a couple of small puffs of pink cloud and stopped.

"All done, Dragon Girls," said the Sky Skimmer,

floating above them. "Better get them back to the Dream Collectors as quickly as you can. Daydreams are best served fresh."

Rosie and her friends didn't need to be told twice. They gathered up the strings of the net and pulled them tight.

The Sky Skimmer led the way out of the head cloud. "Let's take the shortcut," it said.

Instead of popping out of the head cloud's mouth, the way they'd come in, they flew out of its ear.

Rosie thought the head cloud looked quite pleased to have them out!

"Good luck, Dragon Girls," called the Sky

Skimmer as they began to jump away over the springy clouds. "And remember, daydream whenever you can."

"Never fear," chuckled Rosie. "I always do!"

Rosie was very glad Mothew was there to lead the way back to the sunset rays. The cloudscape had completely changed, and she had no idea which way to go.

But Mothew had no trouble finding his way. "I can smell the sunset on the sunset rays," he explained proudly.

They arrived back at the place where the rays poked up through clouds.

"So how do we get back down?" asked Phoebe. "It's very steep!"

"Yes, it's VERY steep!" Mothew agreed cheerily. "But it's also very fun. Just make sure you hold on tight."

Rosie went first. Gripping on to the daydream bubbles with one claw and a gleaming ray with the other, she launched off. The air streamed past her, almost taking her breath away. It was the fastest, most slippery slide she had ever been on! Her heart leapt into her chest, and she let out a happy little roar.

As they neared the treetops, she heard a purry voice in her ear. GlidyCat!

"Get ready to let go of the ray," GlidyCat said. "We will be over the daydream clearing in a moment. Three, two, one! Let go!"

Rosie let go of the ray. For a moment, she tumbled through the air. Then she remembered she had wings. Flapping hard, she righted herself in the sky, still clutching the daydreams.

It felt good to be flying again! She looked over her shoulder and was pleased to see that Phoebe and Stella had let go of their rays and were also flying.

"Goodbye, Night Dragons!" called Mothew and his dad, who were still sliding down the

ray, heading toward the station below. "Thanks for the adventure!"

Down below, Rosie could see the clearing. The newly repaired daydream bubbles began to jostle about, as if they were eager to be set free.

"Nearly there," Rosie said to them soothingly.

A few moments later, Rosie and the others landed back in the clearing. The Dream Collectors came bounding over.

"You did it!" they squeaked. "The daydreams are fixed! Hand them over, and we'll start hiding them in the forest."

Rosie barely had time to undo the net before the squirrelly creatures began grabbing the daydreams, balancing them on their tails, and leaping away into the undergrowth. The net began to uncoil itself and slithered back into a neat knot at the base of Rosie's necklace.

"Am I imagining it," said Stella, "or is it getting darker already?"

Rosie looked around. Stella was right! The golden twilight glow had definitely begun to fade. The rich velvet blue of night was creeping into the sky.

GlidyCat fluttered in midair. "It's time to return to the Tree Queen's glade," she announced.

The twilight colors continued giving way to nighttime shades as Rosie and her friends flew through the forest. Rosie could hear the birds singing their final songs of the day. Animals scampered into their burrows for the night.

Normally, Rosie felt a little sad when twilight faded. But not today! Night falling meant they had succeeded in their quest. *And twilight will return tomorrow*, she reminded herself.

At the edge of the glade, GlidyCat stopped.

"Thanks for all your help," Rosie said. She would be sorry to see the little creature go.

The Night Dragons waved to GlidyCat as they stepped through the shimmering air surrounding the glade.

As elsewhere, nighttime was falling in the glade. The Tree Queen's branches were lit up by dozens of tiny glowworms.

The Tree Queen's branches swayed as Rosie, Phoebe, and Stella moved closer. "Well done, my Night Dragons," she said in her strong, kind voice. "You've achieved the first part of this quest!"

"The *first* part?" repeated Stella. "You mean there's more to do?"

"Yes," replied the queen, a smile in her voice. "You have managed to protect the daydreams from the Fire Queen and allow night to fall. For these things, I am very grateful. But there is more to be done, and I will call you back to the forest before long. That is, if you are prepared to help the Magic Forest again?"

Rosie and her friends answered in one voice. "Of course we are!"

Rosie took off the silver chain and thread and returned it to the Tree Queen.

"Then this is not goodbye, it's just until next time," said the queen, reaching out an elegant branch-arm to retrieve the magical thread from Rosie. "To return to the human realm, look for your bubble outside the glade."

Rosie wasn't quite sure what that meant, but the Tree Queen had already turned back into her tree form.

"Come on," said Stella. "We'll figure it out."

Together, the three friends pushed back out

through the force field. It was almost completely dark now, and quiet. Looking around, Rosie could see that the Dream Collectors had been busy, placing bubbles all around for the forest creatures to find the next day. Most of them were very pale, as if their internal light had been switched off.

But three daydream bubbles glowed brightly. One was bright pink and purple, one was pale blue, and one was a deep purple and yellow. The colors of the Night Dragons!

"Those must be our bubbles," said Phoebe. "The ones to get us home."

Rosie nodded. She had been thinking the same thing.

"See you back at the sleepover," she said to her friends, then turned to the pink-and-purple bubble, which seemed the most beautiful one to her. As she walked toward it, a pink mist rose up around her, swirling and scented faintly with roses.

She closed her eyes and breathed in the scent, feeling the breeze grow stronger and stronger until it lifted her up into the air and spun her around.

〜

A moment later, the breeze eased off, and she drifted down to the ground. Opening her eyes, Rosie found herself back in Phoebe's bathroom. The soapy clouds in the sink were still there!

For a moment, Rosie felt sad. The Magic Forest had been so beautiful. And it was amazing to fly among the clouds!

But then she heard her friends calling from the other room. "Rosie, hurry up! The sun has just set."

Rosie felt a smile spread across her face. They would return to the Magic Forest before long. The Tree Queen needed them.

But right now, she had a sleepover to enjoy.

"Coming!" Rosie called. "Don't eat all the snacks without me!"

Turn the page for a special sneak

peek of Phoebe's adventure!

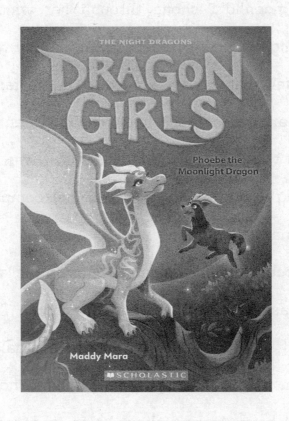

The full moon was rising as Phoebe got ready for bed. Tonight it looked closer than usual. The moonlight shone through her window, bathing her room in a beautiful silvery glow that felt magical. Phoebe wasn't a big fan of the dark. In fact, she hated it! But when the moon was big and round like this, it was like having a night-light on. It kept her company and made her feel safe.

Phoebe put her jeans and T-shirt in the laundry basket and slipped into her pajamas. They were her favorite ones, with a swirling galaxy design. Often when she wore them, Phoebe would have dreams about being in a rocket ship, shooting through space. In these dreams, Phoebe was always with her best friends, Rosie and Stella.

The three girls did everything together, including Sleepover Club most Friday nights. The original idea had been that they'd take turns sleeping at one another's houses, but Phoebe often asked Rosie and Stella to sleep at hers. Sometimes she got homesick, especially in the middle of the night when everything was dark and quiet. She felt more relaxed when Sleepover Club was at her home. Then she could make sure that her bedroom door was open just the right amount so that the light from the hallway filtered in. And secretly, she liked knowing her parents were only a couple of rooms away.

At the most recent sleepover, something very strange had happened. Phoebe, Rosie, and Stella had been transported to a magical forest. And in that forest, they had become Dragon Girls! Not just any dragons, either. They were Night Dragons. Their adventure had been like the best dream ever, except it had actually happened.

Phoebe loved feeling so powerful. She often felt nervous in her normal life, but nothing was scary when you were as strong as a dragon. And the flying! It had been a little difficult at first, but the more she practiced, the better she became. Phoebe often dreamed about flying, so actually doing it was incredible. Especially with her friends by her side.

Phoebe pulled on her robe and went to stand by her window. She opened it so the night air flowed in. It had been a warm day and the evening had yet to cool down completely. Phoebe leaned against her windowsill, looking out over the neighbors' yards.

The Tree Queen, the ruler of the Magic Forest, had told Phoebe and her friends that they would be needed again soon. Phoebe had been worried when she first heard that they were going on a quest. She did not think of herself as brave. But when the Tree Queen explained that the evil Fire Queen was trying to banish nighttime from the Magic Forest, she knew they had to help.

Even though Phoebe didn't like the dark, there were still lots of things she loved about nighttime. Sleepover Club, for instance! Gazing up at the moon each night was wonderful, too, seeing it wax and wane. She also loved snuggling up in her comfy bed and feeling like she was floating on a cloud as she fell asleep. And the way that her dreams took her to all kinds of wild places? That was worth fight-ing for!

As Phoebe looked up at the moon, she noticed

that the moonlight was different somehow. Rather than its usual pale, silvery color, the moonlight was almost aqua.

There was something else strange going on. Phoebe could hear distant singing.

Magic Forest, Magic Forest, come explore…

Phoebe felt a tingle of excitement. She had heard that song when she traveled into the Magic Forest last time! That had been on Friday, a Sleepover Club night. But tonight was Tuesday. Was she about to return to the forest anyway? And would Rosie and Stella be there, too?

ABOUT THE AUTHORS

Maddy Mara is the pen name of Australian creative duo Hilary Rogers and Meredith Badger. Hilary and Meredith have been making children's books together for many years. They love dreaming up new ideas and always have lots of projects bubbling away. When not writing, Hilary can be found cooking weird things or going on long walks, often with Meredith. And Meredith can be found teaching English online all around the world or daydreaming about being able to fly. They both currently live in Melbourne, Australia. Their website is maddymara.com.

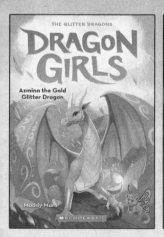

THE TREASURE DRAGONS

DRAGON GIRLS

We are Dragon Girls, hear us ROAR!

Read all three clawsome Treasure Dragon adventures!